PEPPE
THE LAMPLIGHTER

BY ELISA BARTONE
ILLUSTRATIONS BY TED LEWIN

LOTHROP, LEE & SHEPARD BOOKS   NEW YORK

To the memory of my father and grandparents —EB

To the American Dream —TL

Library of Congress Cataloging in Publication Data. Bartone, Elisa. Peppe the lamplighter / by Elisa Bartone ; illustrated by Ted Lewin.   p.   cm.   Summary: Peppe's father is upset when he learns that Peppe has taken a job lighting the gas street lamps in his New York City neighborhood. ISBN 0-688-10268-9.—ISBN 0-688-10269-7 (lib. bdg.) [1. Italian Americans—Fiction. 2. Fathers and sons—Fiction. 3. Brothers and sisters—Fiction. 4. New York (N.Y.)—Fiction.] I. Lewin, Ted, ill. II. Title. PZ7.B28563Pe 1993 [E]—dc20 92-1397 CIP AC

A long time ago when there was no electricity and the streetlamps in Little Italy had to be lit by hand, Peppe lived in a tenement on Mulberry Street. His father was sick and his mother was dead, and so, though he was just a boy, he had to work to help support his sisters: Giulia, Adelina, Nicolina, Angelina, Assunta, Mariuccia, Filomena, and Albina (who lived in Naples with her uncle, the priest, and took care of orphans).

Peppe tried hard to find a job. "I could sweep the floor and put new sawdust down," he told Gennaro, the butcher.

"Sorry, Peppe, business has been slow," Gennaro answered.

"I could wash the glasses!" he told Don Salvatore, the bartender.

"Maybe when you're older, Peppe," said Don Salvatore.

"I could help make the torrone and string the hazel-nuts," he told Commare Antonietta, the candy maker.

"Sorry, Peppe," she answered.

He even went to Fat Mary, the cigar maker. "I could count the cigars and put them in boxes!" he told her. But she didn't need him either.

Then one day he met Domenico, the lamplighter, on the street. "I heard from Don Salvatore that you're looking for a job," the lamplighter said. "I'm going back to Italy to get my wife. Will you light the lamps while I am gone and save my job for me?"

"Oh, yes, Domenico! Thank you!" Peppe answered. Then he ran all the way home, anxious to share his good news.

"Papa! Nicolina! Mariuccia! I have a job!" he shouted. "Beginning tomorrow I will light the streetlamps!"

Nicolina hugged him. Mariuccia kissed his cheeks. Assunta hopped up and down and clapped her hands. But Papa sat silent and still, his face like stone.

"Did I come to America for my son to light the streetlamps?" he said. Then he walked out, slamming the door behind him.

Peppe hung his head.

"Don't mind him," said Filomena.

"He's sick; he doesn't realize what he's saying," said Angelina.

"Papa loves you," said Adelina.

"It's a *good* job, Peppe!" said Assunta.

Peppe tugged gently on Assunta's hair and smiled at them. But he did not really feel like smiling.

Each evening at twilight Peppe took the long stick of the lamplighter and passed through the streets. He reached high for the first streetlamp, poked open the glass, and set the lamp aflame. Then one by one he lit them all—and each one Peppe imagined to be a small flame of promise for the future.

What a joyful feeling it was to light the streetlamps! It was almost like lighting candles in the church for special favors from the saints.

"This one for Giulia, may she have the chance to marry well....

This for Adelina, may she have the dress she likes....

This for work for Nicolina in the biscuit company....

Piecework for Angelina, for many gloves to sew...."

This so that Assunta learns good English in the school....
Good pay to embroider I wish for Mariuccia....
And for Filomena, may she learn to like New York....
This for Albina, for strength to help the orphans....
This for my mother, may she look on us with pleasure....
And this one for Papa, may heaven help his heart!
And this one for me, that I will always be able to help
Domenico light the lamps."

Once when Peppe got home, Papa was watching from the window. "You'll belong to the streets!" he shouted.

Peppe sat on the stoop way past his bedtime, then cried himself to sleep when no one would hear. In the morning his shoulders drooped, just a little.

"Hey, Peppe, don't look so sad!" Fat Mary teased, and Peppe tried not to.

But Papa stayed angry. "You'll never amount to anything," he grumbled.

Giulia took Peppe's hand in hers. "Don't worry about it," she told him.

"Peppe, look up when you walk!" Nicolina reminded him as he left for work.

Peppe tried, but when he came home, Papa turned away. "I don't even want to look at you, you make me so ashamed," he said.

"You never play with me anymore, Peppe," said Assunta.

Peppe just lowered his eyes and didn't answer. And from then on he rushed through the lighting of the lamps, sometimes forgetting which was which.

"It's a stupid job," he said to himself. And he began to imagine that the people of the neighborhood laughed behind his back.

Soon he would not show his face outside the tenement …and one night, the streets of Little Italy were dark. "Where is Peppe the Lamplighter?" said the people to one another.

Peppe sat in the kitchen, his head in his arms. And on that night Assunta did not come home.

Giulia kept glancing out the window. Adelina let the macaroni cook too long. Papa walked back and forth, back and forth. He didn't eat much dinner, and pushed away his coffee without taking one sip.

"Dov' è mia bambina?" they heard him mutter. No matter how big she got, Assunta would always be his baby.

Finally he spoke. "Peppe," he pleaded, "don't be stubborn. Light the lamps!"

Peppe couldn't believe what he was hearing. "But I can't light the lamps, Papa!" he said. "I don't want to belong to the streets. I don't want to grow up to be a beggar. You brought us to America to do better things! I have to study, to be a doctor maybe."

"The streets are dark, Peppe," said Papa. "Assunta is frightened. Tonight the job of lamplighter is an important job....Please, Peppe, light the lamps. You will make me proud."

Peppe could not refuse his father. Quietly he put on his coat and collected his things. Outside he reached high for the first streetlamp and set it aflame. Then one by one he lit them all. Each time he whispered, "May Assunta be safe tonight."

At last, behind the last streetlamp, the one that Peppe always lit for himself, he found her. She huddled against it, unable to move for fear of the dark. He picked her up. "Why didn't you light the lamps for us tonight, Peppe?" she asked.

"I'm sorry, Assunta," he answered.

"Peppe, when I'm bigger I want to be like you. I want to light the streetlamps. I think it must be the best job in America."

"The best job?" said Peppe, wondering.

"You scare the dark away," Assunta told him. Peppe smiled and held her tighter.

He glanced up at the last streetlamp. "You can light this lamp tonight, Assunta." He helped her hold the stick.

On the way home Assunta fell asleep in Peppe's arms. As Peppe walked, he held his head up, and his eyes were bright again.

Peppe walked into the tenement and climbed the stairs to their apartment. Assunta was still sleeping. Six sisters ran to embrace them both. Then they had to make room for their father. For the first time in a long time, he put his hand on Peppe's shoulder. "It's a good job, Peppe," he said. "Light the lamps. You make me proud."

So Peppe lit the streetlamps once again, pretending with all his might that each one was a small flame of promise for tomorrow, like it used to be.